P9-CAN-547

WALT DISNEY PRODUCTIONS
presents

Hiawatha
the Brave Hunter

Random House  New York

Book Club Edition

First American Edition.
Copyright © 1979 by Walt Disney Productions.
All rights reserved under International and
Pan-American Copyright Conventions.
Published in the United States by
Random House, Inc., New York,
and simultaneously in Canada by
Random House of Canada Limited, Toronto.
Originally published in Denmark as
HIAWATHA—DEN TAPRE JAEGER
by Gutenberghus Bladene, Copenhagen.
Copyright © 1978 by Walt Disney Productions.
ISBN: 0–394–84234–0 ISBN: 0–394–94234–5 (lib. bdg.)
Manufactured in the United States of America.
90   A B C D E F G H I J K

Little Hiawatha was a very small
Indian brave.
Every night he listened to the stories
the other Indians told around the campfire.

During the day he listened to
his grandmother, who taught him
many things.

She taught him how to make
a canoe out of birch bark . . .

. . . and how to cook fish.

She also taught Hiawatha
how to find
the North Star,
so he would never
get lost.

She taught him that the animals
of the forest were his friends and
that he should be kind to them.

But Hiawatha often dreamed
he was a great hunter.

One day an older brave said,
"Hiawatha, here is a bow I have made
for you. It is time for you to learn how to hunt."

Hiawatha was so happy.

He danced
a small Indian dance.

And he sang a small Indian
song of joy.

Proudly he showed his new bow
and arrow to all his animal friends.
"Isn't it wonderful?" he said.
"Now I can become a great hunter."
The animals looked very afraid.
"You are not
going to shoot US,
are you?"
they asked.

"No, of course not," said Hiawatha.
"You are my friends. I am going to paddle
my canoe to the island. I will hunt there."
"Be careful," said the animals.
"Hunting can be dangerous!"

"I know what I am doing,"
Hiawatha said as he climbed into the canoe.
"I will show you I am a great hunter!"

But the animals were not sure about that,
so they swam after the canoe to watch out
for him.

"Hiawatha!" the animals cried.
"You are paddling too fast! You are going
to crash into the bank!"

"Be quiet!" said Hiawatha. "I know
what I am doing."

But sure enough, the animals were right.
The little canoe hit the bank,
and Hiawatha fell—SPLAAT!—into the water.

He looked so funny that the animals
could not help laughing.

But Hiawatha did not think it was funny.
He was soaking wet.

"Stop laughing," he said angrily.

When he crawled out of the water,
he saw something that made him forget
he was angry.

He saw animal tracks!

Hiawatha was very excited.
"Follow me," he said to his friends.
"I must see where these tracks lead."

Hiawatha was starting his first
adventure as a hunter.

He followed the tracks until he came
face to face with—a giant grasshopper!

The grasshopper jumped
into the air.
Hiawatha was so surprised
that he fell backward
into a thorny berry bush.

"Ouch!" he cried.
The thorns pricked his skin.

His rabbit friend thought
Hiawatha looked funny.
He laughed and laughed.
"What a brave hunter!" he said.

This made Hiawatha angry again.
"I will show you I am a real hunter,"
he shouted. "You had better run
for your life!"

Hiawatha chased
the rabbit all over
the island.

They ran uphill
and downhill.
"Help!" cried the little rabbit.
He was very frightened.

Hiawatha chased the rabbit
down to the lake.

"Now I have you," he said,
"because you can't swim."

Hiawatha put the arrow
in his bow and aimed it
at the rabbit.

The poor rabbit began to cry.

"Oh, please don't shoot me,"
he begged. "I am sorry I laughed
at you."

Hiawatha forgave him
at once.

He dropped his bow and
gave the little rabbit
a big hug.

He knew he could never
shoot his friend.

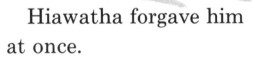

Then he picked up his bow
and arrow and broke them in half.
"I do not want to be a hunter
any more," he said.

"Why don't you
become a scout
instead?" asked
the skunk.

"That's a wonderful idea!" said Hiawatha.
"I will start by scouting the island.
Follow me!"

They had not gone far
when they saw
some more tracks.
These were big ones!

"I don't think we should follow
those tracks," said the mouse. "Those
look like bear tracks!"

But Hiawatha would not listen.
He wanted to follow the tracks.
They led to a cave.
"Look!" said Hiawatha.
"There is a little bear cub."

"Come here, little teddy bear,"
said Hiawatha as he chased after
the bear cub. "I won't hurt you!"

But the bear cub was afraid,
and he ran into the cave.
Hiawatha crawled after him.
"Ha, ha! I can see you!" he said laughing.

But it was not
the little bear cub that
Hiawatha saw.
It was the great big father bear.
"GRRRR!" he growled angrily.
"Help!" cried Hiawatha as he
and his friends ran out of the cave.

Hiawatha ran
as fast as he could,
but the father bear
was right on his heels.

They ran past two beavers
who were cutting down a big tree
with their teeth.

"Run this way," said the beavers
when they saw that Hiawatha was
in trouble.

The beavers quickly
chewed through the tree trunk.
CRASH! Down it fell, right
on top of the big bear's head.
"Hooray!" shouted the beavers.
"You must be more careful,"
the fawn said to Hiawatha. Hiawatha was
holding on to his friend, the rabbit.

Hiawatha picked some flowers
for the two beavers.
"Thank you for saving my life," he said.

"Hiawatha, it is getting late,"
said the skunk. "We should
start home."

But when they reached the shore,
Hiawatha's canoe was gone!

"What am I going to do?" said Hiawatha.
"It is much too far to swim."

The two friendly beavers came running.

"We will find the canoe for you," they said.

But Hiawatha saw the canoe floating out on the lake.

The beavers jumped in the water and
started to swim.

In no time at all, the beavers
reached the canoe and pushed it to shore.
Hiawatha and the animals
danced for joy.

But the paddle for the canoe was missing!

"Don't worry," said the beavers. "We will
think of something."

Hiawatha and the other animals
climbed into the canoe, and the beavers paddled with
their strong wide tails.

Soon the canoe was racing through the water.

"Thank you very much for your help,"
Hiawatha said to the beavers when they landed.

"You are welcome," they said. "Now we
will look for your paddle. It must be
floating out there somewhere."

Hiawatha's grandmother was waiting
for him.

"How is my brave little hunter?"
she asked. "Did you have a good day?"

They sat on a blanket in front of
the tent, and Hiawatha told his grandmother
all about his adventures.

"Do you think I will make a good
Indian scout?" he asked.

"Oh, yes," said his grandmother.

Then it was time for
Hiawatha to go to sleep.
"Good night, little scout,"
said his grandmother,
as she rocked him in his
hammock.

Hiawatha soon fell asleep and
dreamed of all his exciting adventures.